Midnight Mayhem

L. R Burke

For the ladies that said, fuck prince charming, turn the page, your psychopath is waiting for you.

Preface

They say life begins when you are born, but I disagree, life begins when you start *living*.

My life was over before it even began, or so I had thought.

The day I was sentenced to Lakeview was notably the worst day of my life, and that means something coming from someone whose just murdered his own father. The jury viewed me as a cold-blooded psychopathic killer, but the only view I cared about was *hers*.

As it turns out, her *view of me* paved the way for my life here at Lakeview.

Lakeview Asylum is home to the most unstable, psychopathic, criminals this side of the Mason Dixon.

Life in an Asylum is not living, it is simply *existing*. Not to say that life is boring here, because it is far from boring you see. It's the opposite of boring, which arguably makes for an interesting existence.

We craved something more though. We craved a life that we could *live*.

And we intend to live.

One
Colton

October 27th
2027

The wind kicks up, battering against the walls of the Asylum as rain pounds hard against the roof. Lightning skirts across the sky, illuminating the growing smile on my cell mates face.

"It's almost time!" Dean shouts out in a sing-song voice that sends shivers down my spine. The clock from the dayroom bellows out the twelve chimes signaling the dawn of Midnight; it only adds to the sinking feeling in the pit of my stomach.

I've spent my entire adult life here at Lakeview Asylum, waiting and praying for a night like tonight. I was sixteen when they locked me away here, my very pretentious lawyer decided I was better off telling the truth. His idea was solid, and maybe would have worked had someone not paid off, the only person who knew the truth about that night.

Lakeview Asylum is home to the criminally insane. It's the only criminal insane asylum on this side of the country. Lakeview is located deep in the heart of Kentucky, surrounded by miles of dense thick woods.

It's been fourteen years since I was issued

a life sentence here, due to the nature of my crime. I've lived that night over a thousand times and there's not a thing I would change about it. Except maybe, in some alternate life where my actions landed me the girl and not a life sentence in an insane asylum.

"Colt, you ready for this?" Dean punches me in the arm, yanking my attention back to the present.

"Yeah man. Are the others already in place?" I already know the answer, KC and Mason have been reeling for this day since we started planning it.

We lost power exactly five minutes ago, the backup generators never kicked on, just like I had planned. Mayhem ensued once the orderlies realized there was no back up power to keep us locked in our rooms.

Despite my wrongful conviction, everybody else here actually is certifiably insane, and highly dangerous. Including the four other men I've grown close to in the last decade, yet here I am actively executing my escape with them.

We started dismantling the backup power system a couple years back, little by little. We've waited for the last two years for a storm bad enough to knock out the power, granting us the perfect moment to escape this hell hole.

Mason whistles out a signature tune, letting the rest of us know it's time. It takes three minutes for the five of us to make it outside the building unnoticed. Another fifteen minutes for us to cross the safety point, a small back road about two miles through the woods. We all breathe out a sigh of relief once we reach the road on the other side of the dense Kentucky woods surrounding Lakeview.

"Shit man, that was exhilarating." KC shouts out, licking blood off his fingertips. I don't ask where the blood came from, the frantic screams from the staff as we were fleeing told me everything I needed to know.

"Shut the fuck up man. You're gonna get us caught dumb ass." Mason lands a punch to KC's shoulder, his own hands are covered in blood, not surprising considering they do everything together.

Mason and KC are cousins, they landed themselves in Lakeview for slaughtering their whole family on vacation when they were eighteen. Full blown fucking psychos, but they are loyal to each other, almost to a fault.

"Both of you shut the fuck up. Where's your sister with the car man?" My eyes shift, landing on Dean, who's scanning the road.

"I dunno man. I texted her the second the power went out. She should be here by now." About the time he finishes talking, headlights cut through the rain, a small SUV creeps to a stop in front of us.

"Y'all boys need a ride?" The window rolls down, a small woman in her early twenties sits behind the wheel.

"Hell yeah we do, get in boys. This is my sister Samantha." Dean beams, hopping in the front seat beside his sister. They hug quickly as the rest of us pile into her car.

"Sam- no one's called me Samantha since our parents died. I'll drive y'all boys to the

Virginia state line. After that it's up to y'all to find your own ways." Sam speaks matter-of-factly, her dagger like gaze landing on Dean.

"Thanks Sam. We really do appreciate it." Reece stutters from his spot between me and KC. Reece is the quiet type, he's ex-military and has been through some fucked up shit at the hands of our government. Sometimes I forget he's supposed to be crazy, he just seems so normal at times. He really does deserve something more in life.

We settle in for the long drive ahead, the rain pounds hard on the roof, lulling Reece to sleep beside me. My mind wanders back to that night fourteen years ago.

The night I became a killer.

June 11th, 2013

"Colton please don't do anything stupid." Alex begged me to stay out of it, but I'd wiped her tears over that bastard for the last time.

"Just stay here Alex. I'm serious." My voice was tight, my hands shook from anger as I slammed the door, leaving Alex alone in my bedroom.

The stairs shook beneath me as I stomped up them. I didn't care if he heard me coming or not. He had touched her for the last time. My right hand gripped the hunting knife tightly as I twisted the *doorknob to his office with my left. He was sitting at his desk, working on some stupid fucking paperwork like he hadn't just raped his stepdaughter minutes before.*

"Hey Colt, whatcha need buddy?" My name rolled off his tongue so innocently, his ability to act like nothing happened made me sick to my stomach.

"Hey dad, anything you wanna tell me?" My words came out clipped, calmer than I expected them to. He still hadn't looked up at me, if he had he would've seen the knife in my hand.

"Colt, is everything okay? You sound upset." My fathers eyes widened as he looked up, finally taking in the scene in front of him. Me standing over him, knife in hand, mid swing. He didn't get the chance to speak again. The blade slid

across his throat in one swift motion.

"No, dad I'm not upset. I'm fucking livid."

I stared into his eyes, watching the life fade from them as I cut his shirt open, carving the word rapist into his chest. He died before I finished, it didn't stop me though. I wanted the world to know what he had done. What he had been doing to Alex for the past seven years.

"Colton! What have you done!" My stepmother screamed out behind me, her face pale, eyes wide with fear as she took in the scene before her. She stood in the door way, staring at me in horror.

My father's dead body was leaned back in his office chair, throat slit, his white collared shirt drenched in dark red blood. I stepped towards her, ready to explain what happened. She faltered, her eyes landing on the hunting knife still gripped in my hand, and ran out the door.

Tossing the knife to the ground, I ran down the stairs after her. She rushed a crying Alex out the front door, already on the phone with the police. Alex looked back, tears in her eyes, but a small smile on her lips that held me in place. I had done it.

I saved her.

"Thank you." Alex mouthed the words as her mother drug her away from me, running towards the neighbors house. There was no need for them to run, I would never have hurt either of them.

I didn't try to run, there was no point. Instead I just sat at the bottom of the stairs, waiting on the police to come.

"We're here." Sam called out, her car coming to a stop in front of the Welcome to Virgina sign.

"Thanks again for the ride Sam. You two take care of yourselves." I shut the door lightly behind me, nodding to her in thanks.

"I'll miss you boys. Maybe I'll see ya around someday." Dean shuffled from foot to foot.

"What the hell. Bring it in boys. We've done the impossible." KC hollers out. The five of us pile in on each other in one giant group hug.

"Y'all take care of yourselves now. Stay out of trouble." I wasn't sentimental by any means, but these men had become my family over the past decade. I wouldn't be standing here without them.

We all murmured our goodbyes, the four of us waving as Dean and Sam drove off, heading north somewhere. We stuck to the woods, following the road into the nearest town together before we all split ways for good.

A part of me wandered where they would end up, but the logical part of my brain knew better than to stay curious. The less we knew about one another the better. I knew for a fact KC and Mason would stay together, more than likely getting themselves caught due to KC's wildly impulsive behavior. I hoped Reece made it somewhere safe and laid low for a while. He deserves his freedom the most out of all of us.

For me, I had a girl to find. Nothing was going to stand in my way.

I'm coming for you Alex.

Two

Colton

October 31st

It took me less than four hours to track Alex down once I got access to a computer. Part of me had expected her to stay in Tennessee, but I knew better. My trial was too public, there wouldn't have been anywhere in the state where she wouldn't have been recognized. I was shocked to find her in South Carolina though, more specifically right on the beach in Charleston. Alex hated the water.

After a two day bus ride I arrived in Spartanburg, South Carolina. I didn't want to take a direct route to her. My guess is the Feds will be knocking on her door first when they go looking for me. On paper she's the only family I have left.

The drive to Charleston wasn't that bad, roughly three hours or so. I rented a vehicle under a fake name, avoided main roadways and paid for everything with cash. There's no possible way I could be tracked, except through security cameras, but I'm not too worried about that.

The guys and I have been planning our escape for the better part of two years, with the help of Dean's sister we were all able to have a decent amount of cash set aside.

Dean's family comes from money, and as far as I know it's just him and Sam that are left. They had no problem making sure the rest of us were set up for success after our escape. I think that Sam is just as fucked up as Dean, she's just better at hiding it. Something about her set me on edge, at least I wasn't with her very long.

I lucked up right after I reached Charleston. I found an old beat up farm truck with tinted windows for sale. It barely cut into the cash I had, so definitely worth it. Plus it gives me a nice place to sit and watch Alex from afar.

Alex has done well for herself. She has a nice bungalow overlooking the beach, it's secluded on a dead end street. I'm parked across the street from her house, watching as she gets ready for what I can only assume is a Halloween party with some girl. I'm glad she has a friend here, she never had many friends back home.

Alex and her friend take their time getting ready. The other girl is dressed in some slutty costume that does nothing for her. Her blond hair clashes with the black dress that really fits her more like a smock. Even with a push-up bra the poor girl has no cleavage at all. Alex on the other hand, she's fucking stunning.

She steps into my view, admiring herself in the mirror. Her long black hair falls down her back in loose curls. She has on a crop top that exposes her large breasts with a criss cross pattern in the front, fish net stockings that hug her luscious thighs and a plaid skirt that barely covers her ass. I thought she was beautiful when we were just kids, but she's only gotten better with age. Alex Sattorie is no longer a scrawny awkward teenager, no she's everything a man could want.

My cock twitches, pushing tight against the restraint of my jeans as Alex bends over. Her little skirt does nothing to hide her black lace underwear that barely covers her curvaceous ass. I can't wait to rip them off of her with my teeth.

Fuck this woman is going to be the death of me.

Lucky for me it doesn't take long before Alex and her friend are leaving. I slipped a

GPS tracker under both cars in Alex's driveway, when I figure out which one is Alex's I'll remove the other one. I may have been in an asylum for fourteen years, but I damn sure wasn't losing touch with how the world worked outside that godforsaken place. Once they're gone, I check my surroundings, making sure no one sees me entering Alex's house.

I planned to pick the lock on the front door, but a familiar flash of pink catches my eye. Oh sweet Alex, you haven't changed at all. Alex lost her keys so much her freshmen year of high school that her mom bought a hide-a-key turtle for our porch. Alex painted the damn thing bright ass pink so it would stand out to her. My heart twinges at the sight of it after all these years. Another wave of relief rolls over me as I remove the turtles back to reveal her spare key.

Once I'm inside her house I let myself soak in every thing about her new life. Abstract animal art decorates her living room, brightly colored animals stare back at me as I make my way through her house. There's no pictures of her with anyone, no friends, no boyfriend, not even a single picture of her and her mom. That doesn't surprise me though, her mother accused her of lying for years before *the incident*.

Aside from the abstract art there aren't many personalized things in here. Alex's place looks pretty basic. Even her room is simple, with just a queen size bed and dresser with a single night stand by the bed. After careful consideration I find the perfect spot to hide a camera. There's a small corner shelf midway up one wall with an overgrown plant situated on it. Once I'm confident that the camera is hidden well I pull out my phone to check the view on the corresponding app. A perfect view of Alex's bed pops up on my screen. A notification flicks across the top of my phone, letting me know Alex and her friend arrived at their destination. I make quick work of hiding a second camera in her shower head before leaving. I slip the spare key back inside the turtle on my way out, she'll never even know anyone was inside her house.

The guy at the tech store showed me various options for hidden cameras, pushing the waterproof one on me hard. If I hadn't spent the last decade with literal psychopaths he would have gave me the creeps for sure. At least he didn't question what I needed them for, and even threw in a three month free subscription to the live feed service offered by the camera company.

Three

Alex

October 31st

"Emma, why are you so persistent I go to this stupid party? What if Mark's there?" I whined from inside my closet, digging for last years Halloween costume.

"I told you, he's not going to be there and you need to have fun! It's been two months since you left him and all you've done is mope around." Emma pouts as she adjusts her bra, willing her nonexistent cleavage to appear.

"Fine, but if I see Mark I'm leaving." I shout back as I pull out the box that I hope has last years costume in it.

"YES!" Emma shouts.

"I'm only going for you, don't expect me to have any fun." I groan as I dig through the box, sighing when I can't find anything.

"Oh whatever, you say that now, but once you're there you'll have fun. I know you will!" Emma is practically jumping for joy.

"I have nothing to wear!" I huff, throwing myself out on the floor.

"Well, I guess we will improvise." Emma giggles as she steps over me, rummaging through my closet. After a few minutes of digging she leans over me, dangling clothes over me.

"Sexy ghost face! I have my little brothers mask from last year in the trunk of my car still. I'll go grab it and clean it while you get dressed." Emma throws the clothes on the bed before darting out of my room.

I let out a heavy sigh and shove myself to my feet. Emma had to pull out the sluttiest clothes in my closet. A black and white plaid mini skirt, with a criss cross crop top that exposes way to much of my boobs. I remember when I bought this outfit, thinking that I would dress up and surprise Mark. Instead, he just accused me of being a whore and told me I was too pudgy to pull the shirt off.

Emma returns holding the mask in one hand and some fishnet stockings in the other. I let out another heavy sigh as I take the stockings from her.

"I could've just worn a smile and dressed up as a mentally stable version of myself." I joke, trying to lighten the mood as I stare at my reflection in the mirror. My chest is on full display, but so is the pudgy parts of my stomach, and my thick thighs. Mark's words ring through my head, driving my insecurities even deeper.

"Alex, stop. You're fucking sexy as hell. Stop letting what that asshole said get to you. He isn't even man enough to appreciate a goddess when he has one." Emma stands behind me, twirling a strand of my hair in her hands.

"Ugh! Fine, let's just go and get this over with." I groan, stealing one last look at myself before turning to Emma.

"Stop it! You're going to have a great time!" Emma giggles, pulling a pint of vodka out of her purse, almost downing half of it at once.

"One of us needs to be sober to drive us there Emma." I laugh, brushing her off as she tries to hand me the bottle.

Despite my insecurities and resentment of parties, I'm here. Seeing everyone having fun makes me want to cut loose, but I'm afraid Mark will show up.

I haven't seen Mark since I left him two months ago, but I know the second he sees me there will be a fight. I avoided Emma's pre-party shots for that exact reason. I want to be sober until I know for sure he won't be here.

"See I told you, no Mark." Emma shouts out over the music after a few minutes of us just lingering through the crowd.

The party was in full swing when we

arrived. Emma was right, we'd been here almost twenty minutes and I hadn't seen Mark at all. A mutual friend was hosting the party and I really expected him to show up, just to see if I was here. An irrational irritated twinge pulls at my heart, our relationship was toxic as fuck, but he hasn't even tried to get me back, which was very unlike him.

"I'm going to find a drink, I'll be back." I shout to Emma before disappearing into the crowd of drunks.

My anxiety is at an all time high, making me feel insanely hot, despite the very little amount of clothing I'm wearing. I yank off the mask and loop the string through the belt loops of my skirt. My face feels like it's on fire and I haven't even had a drink yet.

My hand collides with someone else's as I

reach for a cup, instantly setting me on edge. Looking up I'm met with a tall masked man staring down at me. He's dressed in all black, wearing a red purge mask. There's something gravitating about him, but I can't place it.

"Hi." Stupid stupid stupid, that's the best you could come up with.

"Hi, yourself." The sound of his voice sets me on fire in ways I've never felt before.

"Sorry, I'm still in your way." Pouring my drink I quickly slide over, giving him space to fix his own.

"You don't have to apologize, you can be in my way any day." The guy leans down to pour his own drink, his face is mere inches from mine and I can't help but notice how intoxicating his scent it.

"Do you... would you wanna dance with

me?" Shit why did I say that.

He doesn't say anything, he just grabs my hand and drags me back to the 'dance floor' in the living room.

His hands roam all over my body as we spin around the room. Something about the way he touches me is euphoric and addictive; I don't want him to stop.

We're well into our second dance together when a fist comes out of no where, slamming into the side of his head with a loud thud. Looking up I'm not surprised to see Mark, shaking his fist, glaring at me.

"What the hell Mark. What are you even doing here?" I scream at Mark, putting myself in front of him, giving the masked mystery man a chance to walk away. Which he does, and not gonna lie, it kinda stung a little. I never even got the chance to know his name.

"Oh yeah, sure turn this around on me. I'm not the one dressed like a goddamn slut, throwing myself at some fucking stranger." Mark shouts as he grips my arm, dragging me towards the door.

Panic rises in my throat as I scan the room for Emma. My stomach twists with nausea when Mark yanks me out the door before I can spot her. He's drunk and this is only going to end one way.

"Mark, we're not even together anymore. You can't act like this." I grind out, forcing my feet to come to a stop.

"The fuck I can't. How many times do I have to tell you Alex, I'm not letting you go. I was fine giving you your space when you were sitting at home sulking. But you don't get to come here dressed like a fucking whore, throwing yourself at strangers. You're mine. Fucking accept it." Mark slurs, his hand tightening around my wrist, yanking me towards him.

"I'm not going with you. I *do not* belong to you." I force out, my heart thundering in my chest. Marks fist connects with my face, a bone crunching sound echoes through my head.

"Shut the fuck up bitch. You'll do as I fucking say." Mark fists his hand in my hair, dragging me towards his car. He tosses me in the front seat, then quickly moves to the drivers side. I don't speak as he throws the car in drive and speeds off.

I wait until he reaches downtown Charleston before making my move. Mark stops at red light, tapping his finger on the wheel in annoyance, waiting on the light to change. I know the second the light changes he's going to take off. My timing is perfect though, I yank the door open and throw myself out as soon as he takes off. I cover my head, tucking myself into a ball as I hit the ground. The metallic taste of blood fills my mouth instantly, followed by a searing pain in my side from colliding with the curb. My vision is hazy, but I force myself to my feet and take off running.

I hit a side street just in time, hiding behind a dumpster as Mark's car rides past slowly. I can barely make him out as he scans the streets looking for me. Luckily it only takes a few minutes before he gives up and drives off.

My blurry vision worsens as I start moving, a stabbing pain shoots through my side, fuck why did I throw myself out so hard. Gripping my side, I force myself to keep moving, I have to get home.

I catch a glimpse of my reflection in the glass of a store front, blood drips from multiple places on my head and my face, my legs and arms are scratched up and already bruising. I look like hell.

I've barely made it to the next street over when a truck comes to a stop beside me. The driver rolls the window down, revealing the same masked man from the party. Something deep down tells me I should run, but I'm too tired to move.

"Get in." The mystery man orders, and for once, instead of fighting, I ignore my instincts and get in.

Four

Colton

November 1st

Dancing with Alex was the highlight of my night, until that piece of shit Mark showed up and ruined it. I had to force myself to walk away, otherwise I risked tearing him apart in a room full of people. That would've definitely got me sent back to Lakeview.

By the time I slip out the back door and make it around to the front, Mark is forcing Alex into his car. She looks calmer than I would expect, she obviously knows how to handle this guy.

To my surprise Mark parked himself directly in front of my truck. He doesn't even look up as I walk past him to my truck. I let him reach the end of the street before I pull off after him.

I'm careful not to get too close to the car in front of me. It takes everything in my power not to ram into his piece of shit Nissan. He stops two red lights ahead of me, just as I'm about to run my light, his turns green. The passenger door is slung open and Alex tucks herself into a ball as she hits the ground.

The breath is knocked from my lungs as I

watch her clamber to her feet and take off running. Pulling my truck to the side, I park, watching from a distance as the fucker turns around after her. He spends less than two minutes searching for her before he speeds off, heading out of town. Movement to my right catches my attention. Alex is clutching her side running down an empty street.

I pull off after her, slowing to a stop beside her, rolling the window down as I call out to her.

"Get in." My voice is tight and commanding. To my surprise she climbs in without any arguments. Alex leans her head against the window, groans of pain piercing the air as she's jostled by a bump in the road. Another bump has her falling over in the seat, more groans of pain echo through the truck with each little bump in the road.

"Everything will be okay Alex. I promise." My words come out softer this time as I push her hair back out of her face.

Blood is smeared all over her, from her head down her arms and even her legs. Within a few minutes she is fully unconscious, sprawled across the front seat of my truck. I debate on taking her to a hospital, but I can't risk getting caught, and dropping off a bloodied unconscious woman is a for sure way to get caught.

Fuck.

After the longest fifteen-minute drive of my life we finally pull back into Alex's driveway. Despite her being unconscious every little bump sent waves of pain through her body, every whimper sent chills down my spine. She doesn't flinch as I scoop her up in my arms and carry her inside. Once again, I'm thanking God for that pink ass turtle.

I rummage through her bathroom for a first aide kit after laying her on her bed. The only thing in here is fucking pill bottles. Lexapro, Zyprexa, Ativan, Trazadone, even fucking Adderall. Fucking hell Alex, I wasn't even on this much shit in the asylum. Moving to the kitchen I almost holler when I find a first aide box under her sink.

Alex is still splayed out on her bed, her

skirt hitched up around her waist, showing off her black lace panties. My cock twitches, growing hard at the sight of her curvy body laid before me like a present. If she wasn't hurting I would take her right now. Just the thought of shoving my cock inside her has me throbbing.

"Fuck, focus you sex deprived moron." My hand slaps across my face hard as I curse myself.

Pulling a pair of scissors out of the first aide kit I cut her shirt and skirt down the middle, exposing her soft skin. She stirs slightly as I rip them the rest of the way off, careful not to jostle her. Her eyes flutter while I work, cleaning up her cuts with alcohol, her side is bruised but doesn't look bad enough to indicate any internal bleeding.

Once I'm done cleaning her up I unhook her bra, pulling it off before moving to slide her panties off. The need to bury my cock in her is overwhelming, but I want her to watch as I come undone for her. I've waited fourteen years for this, it needs to be perfect.

Instead, I climb on her bed between her legs, freeing my cock from my restraining jeans. Gripping my cock with my right hand, I trail my fingers up her thick thighs with my left hand. My cock throbs as I stroke it hard, gripping her thigh and spreading her leg wide. I run a finger through the folds of her pussy, jerking my cock faster. Alex moans softly in her sleep as I rub her clit gently, slipping a finger inside I find she's soaking wet. I pump my finger in and out slowly at first, then faster, slipping another finger in as I work my cock. Her pussy tightens around my fingers, sending me over the edge. My breathing stills as I shoot my cum all over her little pussy. Alex moans softly, her eyes flutter a few times, but she doesn't wake.

"Fuck baby, I can't wait to bury myself inside you. Fill you full of my cum and breed you like the good little slut you are." My finger rubs her clit lazily, smearing my cum in all over her pussy.

Headlights spill through the window as a car pulls into the driveway. A notification pings on my phone letting me know Alex's friend has arrived. Fuck.

"Alex!!! Are you in there? Somebody said they saw you leave with Mark??" The friend bangs her fist against the door, her words heavy with worry.

"Alex!!!??? If you don't open the door in the next five seconds I'm coming in." Shit, can't this bitch just mind her own business. Throwing a blanket over Alex, I zip my pants back up and make my way to the front door just as a key slides in the hole.

"Hi, what is all the screaming about?" I plaster a fake grin on my face, forcing myself to sound cheery. The blond looks up at me as I yank the door open, her eyes wide with shock.

"I uhm. I'm sorry who are you? Where is Alex?" Blondie tries to push past me, letting out a frustrated sigh when I don't budge.

"My names Sawyer, Alex is asleep." I force a softer expression on my face, hoping she is satisfied enough to leave.

"I'm sorry, I don't want to be rude but I

don't know you. I need to see Alex." Blondie shoves past me, she may be scrawny as hell but she's strong for sure.

"Alex!" Blondie shouts down the hall, the most annoying squeaking yell I've ever heard.

"Hey, I said she was asleep. Chill with the fucking shouting would you." I grind out, as I follow her down the hall.

"Oh." Blondie stops short just inside Alex's doorway. Alex is curled up under the blanket, snoring softly.

"See? I told you, safe and sound in her bed asleep. Now could you leave so I can get some sleep too?" My words are harsh as I point towards the front door.

"Yeah, I'm sorry. When I heard she left with Mark I was worried. Wait, how do you know Alex? She has never been the 'bring a stranger home' type." Blondie turns to stare me down, her arms crossed over her chest.

"We grew up together. She did leave with Mark but they got into it. I happened to find her walking downtown. I had planned to grab a hotel and surprise her tomorrow, but fate had other plans." I can't help the sloppy grin that spreads across my face.

"Well, that's good. I hate Mark. I knew she wouldn't have went with him willingly. Thank you for getting her home." Blondie starts to leave but spins around last minute. "Just let her know Emma dropped her phone and keys off and that I was worried about her." She hands me Alex's phone and keys then heads out.

"Thanks Emma." I force myself to sound as friendly as possible, shutting the door behind her.

Once Emma is gone I get busy. Using Alex's face I unlock her phone and start going through everything, app by app. I've got fourteen years of stuff to catch up on.

I'm scrolling through her TikTok videos when a text from *Mark* comes through.

Mark: I'm so sorry I hit you Alex. I just miss you so fucking much baby. Please let's talk about this. You know I didn't mean it. I just get so mad when you deny me like that.

Fucking bastard thinks he can talk his way back into her life with some half assed apology, I think the fuck not. After I delete his text I block him from her phone. She doesn't need that fucker anyways. I spend another thirty minutes going through her phone, making notes of all the important things. Where she works, her favorite places, *Marks house,* and the people she spends the most time with.

Fully satisfied with all the new information, I make sure everything Alex will need in the morning is laid out on her night stand. A fresh bottle of water, extra strength Tylenol, her phone, keys, and extra bandages. After a few minutes of searching through her drawers I find a pen and note pad.

I scrawl out a short note then leave it on her night stand with the Tylenol bottle sitting halfway on it.

Five
Alex
November 2nd

My eyelids flutter open painfully. Between the blinding sunlight streaking through my window and the stabbing throbbing sensation in my head, I'm surprised I can still see. A loud ping from my phone catches my attention, rolling over I grab it off my table, forcing my eyes to focus on the screen.

10:00 a.m., November 2nd, 2027.

Fuck, how have I been out for two days.

A hundred notifications slide across the screen, but it's a text from Emma that chills me to my core.

Emma: Hey girl, please text me, I'm worried about you. That Sawyer guy said you and Mark got into the night of the party. Also, I need all the details about him...he's sexy as hell girl.

Sawyer? Fighting with Mark? My head spins as I struggle to remember what happened Halloween night. Tossing my phone aside I head to the shower. My reflection in the mirror stills me, my naked body is covered in bruises and cuts. What the fuck happened to me? My whole body hurts like I've been hit by a truck. Jesus I'm going to kill Mark for this shit.

The hot water caresses my body, warming and relaxing my stiff, painfully sore muscles. Removing the shower head I ease it between my thighs, to my surprise thats the one spot I don't feel sore. Mark likes to rough me up then fuck me, his sick way of 'showing his love'. Seems like he didn't get the chance this time. Thank God, I don't ever want him to touch me again.

I stay in the shower, enjoying the way the hot water soothes my aches and pains. My head rests against the wall, water falls down my back, forcing me to relax. After only a few minutes the warmth turns to an icy chill, signaling the end of my shower. I rush through washing myself and my hair, cursing myself for not asking the landlord to come fix the damn water heater. After wrapping myself in a towel I flop down on my bed, exhausted from the short walk from the shower to the bed.

I reach for the bottle of water beside my bed, freezing instantly when I notice the hand written note under the Tylenol bottle.

Alex,

Take the Tylenol and stay hydrated. I'll know if you don't. Get as much rest as you can. You'll need all your strength the next time I see you.

- C

A chill runs down my spine as Emma's text replays in my head.

Sawyer... -C.... It couldn't be. Could it? My head spins at the thought...if it was him that means... he saw me naked. The thought has me squirming.

I don't get a chance to process anything further than that, a loud knock interrupts my thoughts. I scramble to find clothes, throwing on the first things I grab, crumpling the note and shoving it in my pocket.

The person on the other side of my door knocks more violently, setting my nerves on fire. Who the fuck is at my door.

"Can I help you?" I yank the door open to find two men dressed in black suits staring down at me.

"Alex Sattorie?" The first man speaks, his words stern, pinning me in place with his hard eyes.

"Y-yes sir. Can I help you?" I stutter over my words, my panic rising quickly, setting my chest alight.

"Yes, I'm Agent Risse, this is Agent

Martinez, we're with the FBI. We're here because your step brother, Mr. Jennings, has escaped from Lakeview Asylum. You're the only family he has left. Have you seen or heard from him Ms. Sattorie?" Agent Risse watches me carefully as I process what he just said.

"N-no. I haven't seen Colton since before...since he was sentenced. When did he escape?" My voice is shaky, memories of green eyes and a deep voice promising me everything would be okay flashes in my head.

"Him and four other inmates escaped last Wednesday, the 27th. As I'm sure you're aware of Ms. Sattorie, Mr. Jennings is highly dangerous and based on personal effects found in his room, highly delusional as well. He hasn't made any progress during his time at Lakeview, after reviewing notes from his sessions with his psychiatrist it is evident that you are the object of his delusions. We are currently unsure if he still remains with his fellow escapees or not. We highly recommend you staying alert and reporting any sighting of him immediately." Agent Martinez pins me with his rough gaze, his hand extended with his card.

"Thank you for letting me know. I'll call you if I see him." My fingers tremble as I take the card, my heart threatening to beat right out of my chest.

"Of course. Stay safe Ms. Sattorie. Oh, and you might want to get that cut on your forehead looked at, it looks slightly infected. We'll be in touch." Risse nods at me as they turn to walk towards their SUV.

What the fuck, as if today couldn't get any weirder.

The sound of my phone ringing jolts me back to reality. Running down the hall I reach my phone just in time to answer before Emma hangs up.

"Hey." My breathing is heavy, my heart still racing from the FBI agents.

"Alex! I've been so worried about you. That Sawyer guy said everything was fine, but then I didn't hear from you yesterday. I was so worried I'd left you in the hands of a psycho killer or something." Emma rambles on, the irony in her words is not lost on me.

"Haha...no of course not. Sawyer is a... a friend I grew up with. We used to be really close. We haven't seen each other in over ten years so I just spent the day with him yesterday. Got some much needed time together." The lie rolls off my tongue effortless, the same way I lied fourteen years ago. The lie that landed him a life sentence to Lakeview.

Emma's voice grows distant as my mind drifts back to that day in court fourteen years ago.

June 24th, 2013

"Ms. Sattorie, can you tell me why we're here today?" The prosecutor asked, his eyes trained on me squirming in my seat

on the stand.

"Yes sir. My step-brother Colton, murdered his father." My eyes flicked to Colton, sitting at the table beside his defense attorney. Colton's eyes met mine, no trace of regret to be found, instead I saw something akin to pride looking back at me.

"Yes ma'am. Mr. Jennings claims that he murdered his father in your defense, Ms. Sattorie. Is that true? Was Mr. Curtis Jennings . raping you as the defense claims?" The prosecutor questions. My gaze wanders to the man in the front row, his arm slung lazily around my mothers shoulders, his eyes pinning me in place, a silent warning to tread carefully. George, my step-fathers brother, the man who would decide what kind of life my mother and I would have after this trial was over.

"N-no sir, he was not." My voice cracks, the air is ripped from my lungs, it takes every ounce of self control not to break down in front of the jury. I can feel Colton's stare on me, his questioning gaze flicks from me to his uncle.

"Can you tell me what it was like living with Mr. Jennings?" The prosecutor gestures towards Colton. Our eyes meet, a single tear falls down my cheek, he just nods at me understandingly before looking away.

"Colton has always been troubled, ever since his mother died when he was nine. When my mother and I moved in with him and his father he acted out severely. He would threaten my mother and myself regularly. As we got older his advances *towards me turned sexual. I had no interest in him that way. My step-father would berate him constantly for his behavior towards me. One day last month Colton accused his father of being with me sexually. The accusation was fueled by the fact that I was finally growing closer to my step-father. I assume Colton became jealous. He started twisting small innocent moments of affection between me and my step-father to match his own delusions."*

My heart cleaved in two as Colton looked up at me, tears sliding down his own face. My stomach twisted as I forced the truth down, burying it deep inside me, like my mother had been forcing me to do for years now.

"Alex, hello? Are you still there?" Emma's shouts bring me back to reality.

"Yeah, sorry I'm just still tired. I haven't slept good lately. Listen I'll talk to you later. I gotta take care of some stuff." I end the call with Emma before she can reply, only partly feeling guilty for lying to her.

Colton is free, and I'm now one hundred percent certain he was here in my house.

Fucking   hell.

Six

Colton

November 2nd

The security camera app on my phone dings, alerting me to movement in Alex's room. Pulling the live feed up I see her sitting on the edge of her bed, looking down at her phone. She looks confused at whatever she's reading, but not enough to deal with it. Instead she stands, taking a moment to stare at herself in the mirror, before getting in the shower.

Alex eases the removable shower head between her thighs, a look of relief washing over her face instantly and I can't help but wonder if she expected to feel discomfort down there. Her shower is over far too quickly, for the both of us. I flick through the live feed back to the view of her bedroom to find her sitting on the bed wrapped in a towel.

I'm enjoying the view of her reading my note, probably racking her brain trying to figure out who left it, when something from the front of her house demands her attention. Alex scrambles to get dressed, shoving my note in her pocket, and disappearing down the hallway. I silently curse myself for not putting up more cameras, whoever is at her door isn't speaking loud enough to be heard. A few minutes later Alex runs back in her room just in time to answer her phone. Her body is shaky from whatever interaction she had while gone.

She doesn't tell Emma the truth about what happened Halloween night. Instead she lies, saying she spent all day yesterday with me. Good girl Alex.

I was shocked when she slept all day yesterday, I fully expected her to wake in excruciating pain. She spent all day, curled up in a ball on her bed though. That's when I set the motion alert on the security app. I wanted to be woken up if she got up through the nigh last night. To my surprise she slept straight through, not waking till this morning. Which is good, she needed all the rest she could get.

Something dark flashes across Alex's face, her eyes lifeless, lost somewhere far away in her own thoughts. The last time I saw that lifeless look in her eyes was the day I was sentenced to life at Lakeview.

Her testimony was my death sentence.

June 24th, 2013

"Colton has always been troubled, since his mother died when he was nine. When my mother and I moved in with him and his father he acted out severely. He would threaten my mother and myself regularly.

As we got older his advances towards me turned sexual. I had no interest in him that way. My step-father would berate him constantly for his behavior towards me. One day last month Colton accused his father of being with me sexually. The accusation was fueled by the fact that I was finally growing closer to my step-father. I assume Colton became jealous, twisting small innocent moments of affection between me and my step-father to match his own delusions." Alex looks to me, her eyes lifeless, glossy with the tears she's trying so hard to hide. Her chest heaves, a single tear falls down her cheek as she struggles to breathe.

"Thank you for your testimony Ms. Sattorie. You're free to get off the stand now." The prosecutor walks forward, *holding a hand out to help her.*

Alex ignores him, making her way off the stand shakily, looking down at the ground as she walks back to her seat. Her mother tries to comfort her, but Alex shakes her off, scooting to the end of the pew. The jury views Alex as some broken girl grieving the tragic loss of her beloved step-father, but I know the truth.

A wicked grin spreads across my uncles face, his arm loosely draped over my step-mother, his vindictive eyes pinning me to my seat. I can't prove it but I know he's behind Alex's false testimony somehow. My guess is it's something do with all my fathers money. That greedy bastard would do anything to ensure he got to keep my fathers fortune.

The prosecutor and my defense attorney

present their closing arguments, but without Alex's testimony supporting my claim, it's useless. It takes less than an hour for the jury to come back with my verdict; guilty. No surprise there.

"We the jury find the defendant, Mr. Colton Sawyer Jennings guilty of first degree murder with malicious intent. Due to the supporting testimony of Ms. Sattorie we agree the defendant is unstable and a danger to other inmates. Therefore we the jury move to have Mr. Jennings sentenced to life at Lakeview Asylum for the criminally insane." The lead juror reads from a notepad, crossing his arms over his chest as he finishes his speech.

"Thank you for your verdict, you may be seated. In light of the violence portrayed in the murder of Mr. Jennings Sr., I sentence *the defendant, Mr. Colton Sawyer Jennings, to a lifetime at Lakeview Asylum for the criminally insane. Court adjourned, bailiff, please take the defendant into custody." The judged slammed his gavel down, sounds of people shuffling outside fill the room.*

Taking one last look at Alex, I find her staring back at me, a solemn expression written on her face.

"I love you." She mouths the words slowly, tears flowing down her face freely now.

Those three little words were what kept me going for fourteen years. I spent six years comforting Alex after my father would abuse her, wiping her tears away, holding her together while he constantly tried to destroy her. Not once in six years did she ever tell me she loved me. I would've killed my father a million times over just to hear her say those three little words.

Groaning sounds snatch my attention back to the live feed on my phone. I'm pleasantly surprised by the view.

Alex is laid across her bed, her legs spread wide as she masturbates. She slides one leg up, working her hips against a bright red vibrator. One hand slips under her shirt, gripping her boobs as she works herself faster against the vibrator. The other leg slides up and her hips come up, rocking fast as she fucks herself hard. Alex cries out, arching her back, her cum spilling out, staining her sheet. She falls back to the bed, runs a finger through her pussy, then brings it to her lips, tasting herself slowly.

My cock throbs hard, pushing against my jeans, as she sucks her cum off her fingers. God she's such a dirty little girl. She's begging to be fucked and she doesn't even know it.

Soon my little deviant, soon.

Seven
Colton
November 2nd

Tracking down Mark was way too easy. His address was saved in Alex's phone. It doesn't look like he's left his house since leaving Alex injured and alone in downtown. He's just a sorry drunk from the looks of it.

I stroll up to his door, my anger already building to dangerous levels. Some fucked up part of brain is enjoying the thrill of this.

"Hello, Mark." My voice is heavy, a devilish grin spreads across my face as Mark opens his door.

"Can I help you?" Mark looks me up and down, scanning for an obvious reason as to why I'm knocking on his door.

"We need to talk Mark. Man to *uhh...piece of shit.*" My gaze slides down Mark, he's a good four inches shorter than me, his hand already curled into a fist at my comment.

"Who the fuck do you think you are." Mark drops his elbow, swinging his fist, but he connects with my palm instead of his intended shot at my face.

"I'm you're worst nightmare *Mark.*" Mark winces as my fingers close around his fist, squeezing till his bones start to snap. Mark stumbles backwards, trying to escape me, but my grip is too tight, he loses his balance instead, falling to the floor. I step forward, standing over him as I kick his door closed behind me.

"What do you want from me?" He cries out, his eyes filling with tears.

"You hurt Alex. I can't just let you get away with that." Reaching in my pocket, I pull out my switch blade. I've got it pressed against Marks throat in one swift motion.

"All this over that fucking whore? Dude you can have her, she doesn't even fuck that good." Mark spits out, his body trembling as my blade presses into his skin.

"See that's where you fucked up Mark. Alex was never yours to begin with, you can't just give something away when it doesn't belong to you in the first place.

She's always been mine. You just couldn't ever make her cum could you, Mark? You're just a pathetic piece of shit who doesn't know what to do with a woman." I trail my blade down Mark's shirt, pressing in hard right above his waist line.

"Man fuck you! You're a sick fuck!" Mark squirms trying to wiggle free, except there's no where for him to go. He's trapped between me and the wall.

"That's the first correct thing you've said since I've been here Mark. I spent a long time locked up with the real crazies of this world. Lets just say I've learned a few things from the best of the best." A wicked grin spreads across my face, his eyes widen as I whirl the tip of my blade around in his shirt.

Mark lets out a vicious cry as I grip his

hand, slicing his fingers off one by one.

"What's wrong Mark? Did you run out of stupid shit to say?" Mark bites down on his lip, his whole body trembles under me as tears stream down is face.

"You look like such a little bitch right now. My own father didn't even cry when I slit his throat. I watched the life fade from his pathetic eyes as I sliced his chest to pieces. And here you are, crying over a few missing fingers." Mark's face turns pale, his eyes gloss over like he might pass out.

"You're no fun Mark! If you pass out I'll have to kill you, and I wanted to have *fun* before killing you!" I pout, poking my bottom lip out for the full effect.

"What the fuck is wrong with you! All this over a fucking bitch!?" Mark shouts, his voice shaky and weak from blood loss.

"See there you go again Mark. You never learn. Let me tell you a little story to help you understand." Mark groans as I pull him up, leaning him against the wall.

"My father married Alex's mother when we were ten, only a year after my own mother died. I hated my father for that, but then I found out he didn't marry my step-mother for her. He married her for *Alex*. My father started touching her for the first time four months after they moved in. I was the *only* person to believe her. I spent *six* years comforting her, and doing my best to protect her. At first I hated my father so much for *hurting* her. But by the time I was thirteen, I hated him for *touching* her. It should've been *me*. I could've made her feel *sooo good,* but she never let me because of *him*." My blade comes up, tilting Mark's chin up, forcing him to look at me. "It took me fourteen years to understand it Mark, but I didn't kill my father that night to *protect* Alex. I killed him that night because I got tired of him touching what was *mine*." Tears fall down Mark's face again, understanding finally setting in as I push the tip of my blade against his throat.

"It's your turn Mark. You've touched what's mine for the last time."

My blade slashes deep into Mark's throat, his blood pours out rapidly. The sounds of him choking on his own blood fills the room instantly. It only lasts a few moments, before the life drains out of him completely.

I move quickly, gathering Mark's loose fingers, before searching his kitchen. I breath a sigh of relief when I find his liquor cabinet. Thank fuck for alcoholics.

"You just made this so much easier on me my friend." I douse Mark's body in the unopened bottle of Vodka from the cabinet.

"Oh Mark, you even have a gas stove. How convenient." I chuckle, snapping a quick picture of Mark's mangled body before turning the stove on.

"I've had fun Mark. I do wish we could've spent more time together though, but my girl awaits."

I pour a line of alcohol from the stove to Mark's body, as well as dousing some of the various things surrounded him. Lighting a cigarette, I take a few drags, then toss it on Mark's body. I stare down at for a few minutes, watching as his body catches fire.

Lucky for me there's no one on the street as I exit his house. It'll take a few minutes before the flames become noticeable to passerby's but I'll be long gone before then.

The drive back to the motel is short. Once I'm settled in I pull out my phone and check on Alex.

She's curled up in her bed reading a book, it doesn't look like she's left her house at all. She was always a homebody though.

Satisfied that Alex isn't going anywhere, I get to work on her present.

Eight
Colton

November 3rd

I spent yesterday afternoon watching Alex from the camera in her room as I worked continuously on her special present. After going back through some of the feed from the last few days I've noticed a few things. One, she hasn't taken her medicine in days, she's only eaten once, and she greatly enjoys masturbating. It's time to change things up a bit.

I wait until she's asleep for the night before slipping through her front door. She's snoring softly as I creep through her house into her room.

"Hello, Alex." My words come out smooth, deep and sultry.

"Colton?" Alex's head snaps up from her pillow, her sleepy eyes searching for me in the dark. "Is it really you?" She raises up, propping herself up on her elbow, rubbing her eyes.

"The one and only baby girl." I yank the cover off her, revealing her luscious curvy body, clothed in a thin black lace night gown.

"What are you doing here?" Alex's fear spikes, her words are shaky as I climb on top of her.

"I missed you Alex, I missed you so much it hurt baby. Fourteen years, I thought of you every second of every day for fourteen fucking years." I knock Alex's legs open, spreading them wide with my knees. Alex squirms under me, my gaze travels down her body, my cock twitches as I take in her bare pussy.

"Colton get the fuck off me. What the fuck is wrong with you." Alex struggles, trying to force her legs closed, shooting daggers at me with her eyes.

"Oh Alex, don't ask rhetorical questions. It's futile." I drag a finger up the inside of her thigh, her eyes widen as I move closer to her pussy.

"I'm serious Colton. Get off of me!" Alex shouts, crawling backwards, her eyes scanning the room when she backs into the headboard.

"Have you forgotten something Alex? I know what you sound like when you really mean no." A wicked grin spreads across my face. My hands grip Alex's thighs, dragging her back to me, pinning her legs wide open.

"Colt. Don't do this." Alex's breathing quickens, her eyes wide with fear.

"You don't understand Alex. I've waited *seventeen years* for this." Her eyes meet mine, watching me as I run a finger between her pussy lips. She's already so wet for me. Alex watches me carefully, gasping when I shove a finger inside her.

"Colton I said stop. This isn't right." A tear slides down Alex's face.

"I heard him fuck you for years Alex. I remember how he would hit you for not being wet for him. The terror in your voice when you would *beg* him not to touch you. How you would fight back against him, slapping and kicking until he would tie you down." I pump my finger inside her slowly, playing in her wetness. "Tell me what you're so afraid of Alex. You're soaking wet for me baby, yet you deny me. Why?"

"Colton, you're my step-brother. This isn't right." Alex shakes her head, but doesn't fight me when I push her legs further apart.

"We're not family Alex. We stopped being family the day I slit my fathers throat. The only thing wrong about this is how hard you're trying to fight it right now." Unzipping my pants, I free my cock, gripping it tight, stroking myself as I finger Alex.

"Colton, I've always thought of you as my step-brother. You saved me from that monster. I was heartbroken when they took you away." Alex chokes back a moan, making another futile attempt to escape me. My finger curls inside her, hitting the most sensitive spot, holding her in place.

"I would believe you Alex. Except, I feel how soaked you are for me baby girl. You can't deny that. You were wet before I even touched you." Pulling my finger free, I lick her cum off, savoring the way she tastes, before shoving my throbbing cock inside her.

"Colton! This is so wrong." Alex cries out, choking back her moans.

"If you really think of me as a brother, then you're just as fucked up as I am. I feel you coming all over me Alex." I drop my head level to hers, whispering the last part in her ear, thrusting into her faster.

"Please...Colton.." Alex cries out.

"You're such a dirty little slut Alex. Look at you, letting your step-brother fuck you senseless."

I grip her thighs hard, guiding her legs over my shoulders, fucking into her harder. Her walls clench tight around my cock, her legs lock around my neck, shaking with each thrust. Explosive liquid leaks out as Alex squirts on my cock, her walls clenching tight around me, milking my own orgasm out. My cock throbs, shooting my cum inside Alex's perfect little pussy.

"Fuck Alex, you look so fucking beautiful with my cum inside you. Imagine how beautiful you'll look carrying our child." My fingers move lazily up and down Alex's legs, she looks like a goddess laid before me. My cock throbs gently inside her, holding my cum inside her.

"Colton...." Alex's face falters, my name is laced with the kind of pain that makes my own chest ache.

"Shhh baby, it's okay. Talk to me, what's wrong." My hands grip her hips, holding her in place.

"I can't have kids Colton." She murmurs the words so softly I almost don't hear them at first.

"What do you mean you can't have kids Alex?" I question, fighting back the gnawing ache in my chest. The pain growing in Alex's eyes isn't enough to prepare me for what she's about to say.

"Your uncle, George, he uhm was like your father in more ways than one. He flashed all the money he inherited after your fathers death, and my mother went running. About six months after the trial ended I fell pregnant. I had no one to help me...no one to protect me from him. He had an abortion scheduled and paid off the Doctor to preform a full hysterectomy. I didn't find out until my first gynecology appointment after high school. They told me I would experience a loss of my period for a while after the abortion." Tears stream down Alex's face as she details the horror my uncle put her through.

If I had known what would happen to Alex I would have planned better, we would have run far away. Where I could protect her. I failed her, I let my selfishness get in the way. I should have planned better.

A loud knock at the front door has us

both jumping, dragging me back from my growing self-hatred.

"Expecting anyone?" I look down at Alex, her wide eyes staring back up at me, shaking her head no.

"I would get it, but I'm a wanted man baby. Probably best that you greet our guest first." I try my best to hide my emotions, best not to let Alex see that side of me yet.

Alex glares at me, wiping her eyes as she gets up. She wraps herself in her blanket, before going to answer the door. Another round of obnoxious knocking erupts through the air right before Alex yanks the door open.

"Can I help you.... officer?" Alex's anger trails off, turning to surprise instantly.

"Yes ma'am. Are you Ms. Alex Sattorie?"

The officer questions. I hate the way he says her name, stupid prick is probably imagining what's under her blanket.

"Yes sir. Is there anything I can do for you this late at night?" Alex's frustration has returned.

"I'm sorry to bother you this late, but I'm here about your ex-boyfriend Marcus Cassidy. He was a victim in a house fire yesterday." The officer explains.

"I'm sorry, if his house caught fire yesterday, why are you just now knocking on my door at almost midnight the next day?" I can fully visualize the way Alex is glaring at this fucker right now.

"Well ma'am, we just got the autopsy results in an hour ago. It seems as if Mr. Cassidy was dead before the fire started. We have reason to believe he may have been murdered." The officer's voice is grim.

"I see..." Alex's voice trails off.

"Ms. Sattorie we need to know where you were yesterday afternoon?" The cop questions, his voice hardening in a way that sets me on fire.

"I was home all day yesterday. Why are you asking me this?" Alex grinds out.

"Due to the violent nature of your previous relationship with Mr. Cassidy we have to rule you out as a suspect. You have the motive to want him dead." The officer speaks firmly. Well maybe if the justice system would do their fucking jobs these piece of shit men wouldn't exist.

"Right. Right. I see how it is. A few police reports of him beating the shit out of me and you fuckers doing nothing about it, makes me your first suspect. I didn't fucking kill him but I'm glad he's dead." Alex slams the door in the officers face, her steps heavy as she comes down the hall.

Always so fucking feisty.

Nine
Alex
November 4th

"First the Feds now the county, I wish they would just go the fuck away." I curse, throwing myself back on my bed.

"Wait, when did the Feds show up? Colton's voice is tight.

"Yesterday, wait no, shit my days are running together. Day before yesterday."

My eyes blur as I try to focus on my phone screen, the clock reads 12:07 a.m. I have to fix my sleep schedule.

"What did you tell them?" Colton questions, moving to sit beside me.

"That I hadn't seen you and I would call them if I did." I reach forward, grabbing the card Agent Martinez gave me, handing it to Colton.

"Well shit, why did you hang on to it baby?" Colton pins me with his eyes, pain written all over his face.

"I'm not going to turn you in okay. I mean maybe I thought about it for a minute, but I couldn't bring myself to do it." I advert my gaze, hiding my bleary eyes from him.

"Why?" Colton's fingers grip my chin, forcing me to look at him.

"I... I don't know. I was forced to lie that

day, I thought I would never get to see you again. I wasn't going to be responsible for sending you back there again." My chest feels tight, constricting my air flow. I hope he can see everything I'm too afraid to say.

"I see. Well, thank you for not turning me in." Colton's lip twists up in a smile, but it doesn't quiet reach his eyes.

"You should probably go now. If the Feds get wind of Marks death they might start snooping around more." The words burn coming out, they're so far from what I really want to say.

"Right. Well, I brought you a present. Don't open it until I'm gone though." Colton stands, moving to grab a small box from his backpack. He sits the box on my nightstand before leaning over me. His hand fists in my hair, pulling me up to him.

His lips crash into mine, ravaging me, leaving me breathless.

"Colton...did you...were you really trying to knock me up or was it just the sex high talking?" I almost regret my question before even asking, but I need to know his answer.

"I am so sorry that fucking bastard ripped that option away from you. Forget what I or any other man wants. He took away something from you before you ever got to decide if you wanted it or not. For that he is spending his eternity burning in hell." Colton places a quick kiss on my forehead before he disappears, leaving me to sit with the weight of his words.

Grabbing the box he left on my table, I open it to find something wrapped in black parchment paper nestled in a bed of red tissue paper. I carefully unwrap the black paper, gasping when I realize what it is.

A thin black piece of twine with three skeleton fingers dangling from it. I shriek, dropping it instantly.

There's a bright pink slip of paper sticking out behind the sea of red. I'm almost afraid to pick it up, but curiosity gets the best of me.

Alex,

It's been fourteen years, but I'll always protect you. Mark can't hurt you anymore.

-love C

Jesus fucking Christ. What is wrong with him.

I pick up the card Agent Martinez left,

debating on calling him. Part of me wants to turn Colton in immediately, but something tugs at my heart, forcing me to hide the card in my night stand.

Despite all the fucked up shit Colton has done, I refuse to turn him in. I won't be the reason he goes back to that place. Even if it means I'm technically harboring a fugitive.

Ten

Colton

November 4th

I watch as Alex opens her gift, her face paling in horror as she realizes what she's holding. She drops the necklace I made her, reading the note with tear filled eyes.

Alex pulls out the card from the FBI agents. She stares at it for a long minute, a weird look on her face that causes my breath to catch in my throat. I'm fully convinced she's about to turn me in. The second she does I'll have to disappear, and leave her behind.

I cannot go back to Lakeview.

To my surprise she puts the card back in her nightstand along with the box and her present. I'm not sure what's going through her head right now, but I'm confident that I can fully trust that Alex will not send me back to the Asylum. Whether her choice is driven by her guilt for sending me there in the first place, or if it's from a desire to have me back in her life is still unclear.

I put my phone away and drive back to my motel in silence. I was always a little fucked up in the head, especially after my mom died, but I never thought I would reach the point of stalking the woman I love. I especially never thought I would be leaving a dead mans bones as a gift for her. The killing doesn't necessarily bother me, it's the way Alex drives me to complete insanity that sets me alight. If my mom could see me now she would have a fit. Then again if my mom was alive today...maybe I wouldn't even be in this predicament in the first place.

I long for a life where I could've met Alex at school maybe. A life where we would've become friends and she would've fell in love with me over time. In a different life Alex and I could be a normal married couple with a few kids running around. In a different life neither Alex or myself would have experienced the kind of trauma we were forced to go through at such a young age. A different life doesn't exist though.

Where are stuck in this life, where I am the monster and Alex is my prey.

Blue and red lights flash behind me, dragging me from my thoughts. For a split second I almost floor it, but it's easier to run on foot from one, than it is to hide from a dozen during a high speed chase. I ease my truck to the shoulder and wait for the officer to approach my window.

"Sorry for stopping you so late son, but I just wanted to let you know you had a taillight out." The officer points to my tailgate, eyeing me up and down suspiciously.

"Thank you officer, I'll be sure to get that fixed right away." I force out, trying not to let my rising fear show.

"Where you heading at this time of night anyways?" He questions, his gaze searching inside my truck for anything suspicious.

"Just heading back home from my girlfriends house. Do you need to see my insurance and registration officer?" The words roll right off my tongue effortlessly, a warming smile spreads across my face

"Nah, that won't be necessary. You just be safe out there and get that taillight fixed. If I see you out again and it's not fixed I'll issue you a ticket. Have a good night." The officer tips his hat, then slowly walks back to his cruiser, inspecting every inch of my truck along the way.

I wait for him to pull off, breathing a huge sigh of relief once he's out of sight. That was fucking close. Luckily my motel is only one street over.

The short five minute drive feels like it drags on for hours. My heart pounded heavy in my chest the entire drive back to my motel.

Once I'm safe back in my room I pull out my phone and check on Alex.

She's tucked in bed under her covers but I can tell she's masturbating. The way she tilts her head back moaning as she bucks her hips is mesmerizing. She kicks the blanket off, her hand moving faster as she nears her orgasm. Something silver catches my eye and I zoom in on her hand working over her pussy.

My heart stops beating and I forget how to breath for a moment. Alex is fucking herself with a knife. Not just any knife, a knife identical to the one I killed my father with.

Alex grips the dull part of the blade between her fingers as she rams the hilt inside her over and over. Her legs start to shake as she squirts all her the blade. My name falls from her mouth over and over, mixed with breathless moans.

I exit the live feed and playback the last five minutes. The way she moans my name lights me up from the inside out. Freeing my cock I ravenously start jerking myself as I repeatedly watch Alex fuck herself with the knife. I'm so entranced by the way she moves and how my name sounds coming out of her mouth that I don't even realize I've blown my load all over my pants.

If there was ever a doubt that Alex was refusing to turn me in simply out of guilt, it's gone now. It was one thing making her cum while *I* fucked it, but watching her fuck herself to thoughts of me, it's absolutely fucking exhilarating.

It's been about fifteen minutes since I checked the live feed, and Alex is still fucking herself hard. My little deviant loves to pleasure herself. She must be nearing her breaking point though because she starts to slow down her movements, her breathing is already jagged and rough from how hard she's been fucking her tight little cunt.

She finally stills, leaning her head back against the wall. Small waves of pleasure crash into her for another few minutes. Little twitches ravage her body as she rides out the fading high of her pleasure. Alex can hardly raise her hand up to turn her lamp off, she doesn't even both to put her knife away. She's drifting off to sleep the second her head hits the pillow.

I lay in bed staring at my ceiling,

dreaming of the day when Alex is wrapped in my arms every night. Craving a future where we can be together without fear of a deathly prosecution against our love. A future where Alex is walking barefoot in our kitchen, pregnant with a little Colt, or a baby Alexis. A future where our love grows abundantly, sprouting through the very fiber of our beings, intertwining our souls for an eternity.

I long for a future that does not exist. A future that a monster ripped right out of Alex's hands before she was even able to want it. I wish I could have taken him out, a car wreck wasn't enough. He should have suffered for what he did to her.

Alex lets out a soft moan, followed by the softest whisper of my name. She longs for me on a deeper level than she's willing to admit, her soul is pushing her towards me rather she wishes it to or not.

Sooner or later you will succumb to your fate Alex.

Eleven
Alex
November 4th

I woke to the sharp rays of sun piercing into my room, my skin still clammy from the fitful sleep I endured throughout the night.

Visions of alternate universes where Colton and I lived out cute cookie-cutter happy ever after's haunted my dreams. I tossed and turned as I watched each beautiful life play out before my eyes, one after another. Falling through each lifetime, desperate to catch hold of one and make it into our realty; tormented to grieve as each one slipped painfully through my fingertips.

Colton has embedded himself so deep into my soul that I don't know if I can ever get him out. What is more terrifying though, is the thought that I might not want to get him out of me.

What kind of person does that make me?

He murdered someone for me, not once but twice now.

Yet, I'm the reason he was sentence to Lakeview with all of those truly insane criminals that have clearly driven Colton to madness.

So should I not feel indebted to him in

some way?

Should I not owe my entire life to Colton for what he did for me, for how he saved me from losing myself entirely to the monster that was his father?

Should I hate him for the hell his uncle put me through after his trial?

Or, should I thank him for showing me how to deal with monsters like them.

Colton may never know the truth of what happened to his uncle. I will take that secret to my grave.

Would I have met the same cruel fate at his fathers hands? Curtis was cruel, far more rough with me than George was. I feel as though Curtis would have forced me to carry out an unwanted pregnancy. No matter what I would have had my choice and my rights ripped away.

These thoughts harass me, one violent assault after another, crashing into me with bone crunching force.

I can't stop the downward spiral that follows. The air is ripped from my lungs as my chest collapses. My bedroom walls close in on me from all sides, pressing tighter until I feel my body start to break from the inside out.

My mind is a war zone and my past is the arsenal that supplies the weapons. Systematically tearing me apart with each calculated memory of the horrors I'm forced to relive. The visions of hands touching me in unwelcoming ways violently rip through me with same force that was used to make me comply.

I'm locked in the hell of my own mind with no way to escape. Fighting to claw my way back from the depths of these horrors.

They tell you in therapy to ground yourself, recommending the 54321 method, or to use 'grounding objects'. But how do you do that when you're frozen in place? When the horrors of your mind take over, holding you hostage.

How do you ground yourself when you can't even find the ground.

Twelve

Colton

November 4th

Screams pierce the air of my motel room, jerking me awake. I fumble with the sheets as I search for my phone. Alex's screams are volatile, making my heart race. My phone hits the floor as I fling my pillow out of bed. I quickly grab it, almost afraid to see whatever has Alex so terrified.

My heart lands in my stomach as my eyes

take in the scene in Alex's bedroom.

Alex is curled in a tight ball in the corner of her room screaming non-stop cries of hysteria. Her nightstand has been knocked over, her mattress is flipped up on it's side, and her drawers have all been pulled out of her dresser.

I throw my pants on and run out the door shirtless and barefoot. It's a struggle to stay within the speed limit. I need to get to Alex, but I'm no use to her if I get arrested.

Unlike the drive last night that felt like a life time, I feel as if I've just cut through time and space in the matter of seconds to get to Alex.

I almost shatter the damn turtle as I yank it open to get to the spare key. She's still in a ball screaming when I finally reach her. Her body is trembling as I drop to the ground beside her, pulling her into my arms.

"Shhh, Alex it's okay baby. You're safe. I've got you now." My voice is soft as I try to soothe Alex over her screams.

I hold her close to me, rocking us back and forth as I continue to soothe her with my words. Her screaming starts to quieten after a few minutes, fully subsiding after about fifteen minutes. The trembling doesn't stop though.

Holding Alex's trembling body close to mine breaks me in more ways than I thought possible. To see her fall apart like this, knowing that I failed to protect her from the nightmares of her past is killing me. I would rip my own heart out of my chest if it meant she never had to go through this again.

I hold Alex for hours, rocking us gently as she works through the last of her episode. When you live in an Insane Asylum it's easy to recognize a PTSD episode when you see one. Reese used to have severe episodes similar to this. He would trash his room, beat the shit out of himself, and then pass out for a few hours. He never would remember his outbursts though, it's like as soon as it came out he blacked out.

It's dark by the time Alex wakes up. I had laid her on the couch earlier so I could put her room back in order. She's waking up just in time too, I ordered some dinner for us, it'll be here any minute.

"Welcome back baby."

Alex jumps at the sound of my voice, frantically looking around until her eyes land on me at the end of the couch.

"Colton, what the fuck. You scared me." Alex's body relaxes a little, she's still on edge though.

"I didn't mean to scare you baby." I reach my hand out in an effort to comfort her, but she just pulls away from me.

"Colton, how do you keep getting into my house?" Alex's eyes scan the room, as if she's looking for the next thing thats going to jump out at her.

"The turtle. I recognized it instantly. Old habits die hard I guess." I toss a half crooked smile at her, hoping she doesn't push any further.

"Why are you here Colton?" Anger rises in Alex's voice, her dagger like gaze pinning me in place.

"You needed help. I came to help." My

response is simple, yet doesn't seem to please Alex in the slightest.

"I don't mean like right now, I mean why did you come find me. Wait- what do you mean 'I needed help', how did you know that?" Alex stands up, backing away from me slowly.

"You called me, don't you remember Alex?" The lie rolls of my tongue before I can even think about it and I regret it instantly.

"No I didn't Colton. I don't even have your number. I'm going to ask you one more time, how did you know I needed help?" Alex's face tells me everything I need to know. The way her furrowed brows pinch together over her slitted eyes is actually quiet frightening in a way.

"Alex, I need you not to freak out when I

tell you this. It's important that you remain calm, do you understand?" I push to my feet, slowly easing closer to her.

Alex opens her mouth to speak but is cut off by someone banging at the front door.

"Alex if you don't open this door right now I'm coming in!" Emma shouts from outside, her voice frantic and filled with worry.

Alex rushes to the door, motioning for me to hide behind it.

"Emma, now's not really a good time. Is everything okay?" Alex is careful to only open the door halfway, but its futile when Emma shoves her way inside.

"Is everything okay?? What the fuck, you're the one who hasn't answered any of my hundred calls or texts. And then my mom calls me worried because the DA just petitioned Judge Karmack for a warrant to search your house. What the fuck is going on Alex?" Emma hasn't noticed me yet, her full attention is on Alex, who is now looking frantically between me and Emma.

"What...when? Do you know why?" Alex's voice is full of fear, her wide eyes are bouncing all over the room. This is not good for her, especially this soon after an episode as bad as hers.

"Less than an hour ago, and I think it's in connection to Mark's death maybe. Karmack had a late court hearing so he hasn't approved it yet, but he's never denied a search warrant before according to my mom." Emma explains, moving to sit down only to shriek when she notices me.

"Emma it's okay, he's a friend." Alex tries to interject but I can already see the wheels turning as Emma starts to figure out who I am.

"You're Colton Jennings, one of the five escapees from Lakeview. It's all over the news." Emma's hand instantly flies up, covering her mouth in shock as she backs away from me slowly.

"I'm not going to hurt you Emma. Just calm down." I keep my voice low and soft, careful to stay extremely still so as not to frighten her anymore than she already is.

"Emma, you don't understand. Whatever you think you know, you don't. You need to leave. Right now though. If the cops show up they will think you knew where he was the whole time. You'll be an accessory at best, but they could get you for harboring a fugitive. That won't look good on your mom at all. So just go home, pretend like none of this happened. I'll call you tomorrow, okay?" Alex grabs Emma, ushering her back out the door as she

To my surprise Emma doesn't argue. She lets Alex coax her out the door, probably in too much shock to argue. Alex turns to me with fear in her eyes, only letting her tears flow once the door is fully shut.

"Colton, you have to go now." Something breaks in Alex, there's a pain I've never seen in her before.

"Come with me Alex." It's not a question and she doesn't have a choice either way. I just want it to be her choice, it will make things so much easier in the end if it is.

"I can't Colton." Tears stream down her face as she looks up at me through her tear filled eyes.

"I was afraid you would say that."

Thirteen

Alex

November 6th

Searing pain shoots through my head as I fight to open my eyes. Everything feels wrong. My body feels too heavy and my mind feels too far away.

"Welcome back sunshine." Colton's voice cuts through the hazy fog clouding my head. My vision still doesn't want to cooperate. Colton's head is fuzzy, almost glitching as he moves towards me.

"Colton...wh-what happened?" My throat is so dry it hurts to speak.

"That's not important right now baby. Let's focus on getting you hydrated and some food in you first. You've been out for almost two whole days." Colton's voice is soothing as he brings a straw to my lips, encouraging me to drink.

Colton helps me into a more upright position before positioning himself beside me. My vision is slowly getting better, everything is still slightly fuzzy, but I can make out most of my surroundings now.

We're in a dimly light room, the only light coming from the small lamp on the table beside us. There's no TV, only the bed we're sitting on, a single nightstand, and a small refrigerator.

"Eat." Colton orders, shoving a spoon full of soup in my mouth.

The hot liquid slides down my throat, soothing the dry scratchy feeling thats been driving me crazy since I woke up. It's eerily quiet as Colton continues to feed me.

There's no noise from outside our room either. None of the typical highway traffic noise, or the bustle of other people coming and going from their rooms. Wherever we are, its got to be secluded.

The pain in my head is finally easing up to a manageable point and my vision is pretty much back to normal. It's a miracle what a little nutrition and hydration can do for you.

"Colton, you've fed me and made me hydrate. Now could you please tell me where we are." I look up at him waiting for his response, but all I'm met with is fear.

Colton stares down at me, his eyes swimming with a thousand words he refuses to say. I swear I see tears welling up in his eyes until he blinks them away.

"Alex, what's the last thing you remember?" His voice is shaky, and I can tell he's struggling to force his words out.

"I don't know. What day is it?" My memory is hazy, but if I focus hard enough I can remember bits and pieces of things, but so much has happened recently I can't grasp an accurate time line for all the chaos.

"Uhm, it's November 6th." Colton breathes out a heavy sigh, his heavy eyes are glued to mine as I try to fit all my pieces back together.

"Emma, I remember talking to Emma. You were there, and she recognized you. Oh my God, you didn't kill Emma did you?" My heart starts racing at the thought.

"No I did not kill Emma. I can assure you she is quiet safe." Colton squeezes my thigh in an attempt to reassure me, but something still feels off.

The vague responses he's giving, the dark secluded room we're in, his jumpy demeanor. It's all adding up now.

"Colton, oh my god, you kidnapped me!" I shout, shoving him away from me as I jump to my feet.

"Alex, it's not what you think…" Colton stands, reaching for me across the bed.

Panic sets in and I bolt for the door.

Colton is on me in seconds though. His rough hands seize my body, stopping me in my tracks. My brain is yelling at me to run, but my body craves his touch in a primal way I can't even begin to understand.

"Alex, if you run I will catch you. There is no body around for hundreds of miles." Colton's breath is hot in my ear, his voice sends shivers down my spine in a bone chilling, pleasure driven way that rocks me to my core.

"Fuck you Colton." Before I know it I've kneed him in the groin. He releases me instantly and I don't hesitate as I dart out the door.

Colton was right though, there's nothing but dense trees in every direction. My odds are slim, but I won't give up without a fight.

My adrenaline takes over, spiking to an all-time high as I run through the dark forest. The pain in my head returns,

The Asylum Boys

growing more intense as I push myself further away from the cabin. My feet ache as I pound my bare soles faster against the rough forest floor.

"Alex, this is futile. You're only going to injure yourself further. Save us both the trouble and come back to me." Colton calls out, his voice echoes from every direction, making it impossible to pinpoint his location.

Everything looks the same no matter which way I go. I must have gotten turned around because the cabin comes back into view as I burst through another clearing of trees. It's the last thing I see before I'm pushed down.

Something cold presses against my throat and I don't have to guess to know it's a blade. Every alarm in my head is ringing at full volume. Colton has never hurt me on purpose, but that was the old Colton. The realization that I'm stuck in a secluded forest with an insane criminal escapee crashes into me like a wrecking ball.

"Colton, what are you planning on doing?" I ask softly, forcing myself to tread lightly. My fiery attitude won't do me any good if it sets him off.

"Alex, I'm not going to hurt you baby." Colton whispers the words as if there's a million people around and no one but me is supposed to hear them.

My breath catches in my throat as he drags the knife down my shirt. He's careful not to press the blade too hard, instead he makes a small cut at the bottom of my shirt, ripping it fully open with his hands.

Colton presses his fingers to my lips, but

there's no need for him to silence me. My rising fear has me choking back any fight I have left in me.

I watch carefully as Colton slides my pants off. Once again, my body betrays my mind as I feel myself getting wet. Colton cuts my panties off and I nearly choke as I recognize the blade in his hand.

Frozen with fear, or maybe lust, I can't tell the difference between the two at this point, I'm forced to watch as Colton uses me like a toy. He runs the blade up and down my thighs, pressing the tip against my skin in various places. My body continues to betray me as I let out a loud moan. There's something quite exhilarating about living out your darkest fantasies with someone who absolutely terrifies you.

"You know you want me just as bad as I

want you. Why do you continue to deny me Alex? To deny us?" Colton's eyes are filled with pain as he stares down at me and for the first time ever, I see the truth hidden behind his eyes.

"When did you know Colton?" I choke out, almost afraid to know his answer.

"Tell me how you got *this* knife Alex." Colton counters, digging the tip of the blade into my thigh. Blood dribbles don't my thigh, but I refuse to allow him to see any sort of reaction out of me. He doesn't deserve it.

"George, he got it back a few years after the trial. I found it in a box of his shit after he died. Decided to keep it as a trophy of sorts I suppose." I spit back at him.

Colton takes a deep breath, his hold on me loosening ever so slightly. Something in his eyes shift and I have this sinking feeling that nothing will ever be the same after what comes next.

"We were thirteen. I found you down by the lake, crying over that fucking bastard again. I held you until you cried yourself to sleep in my lap. Thats the day I fell in love with you Alex. The day I knew I would do anything to make you happy. That's the day I decided I would end your suffering at his hands. I didn't know when or how, and believe me, killing him wasn't at the top of the list then, but I knew one day I would protect you from him for good." Colton's chest heaves as he physically releases those words, he's held onto for all these years.

"Colt..." I don't know what else to say, my feelings for Colton are complicated, I'm not even sure I could put them into words even if I tried. So instead of trying, I just kiss him.

Our mouths collide together in a clash of teeth and tongues. Colton ravages my mouth, taking every piece of me that I freely give him. I let out a cry of pleasure as he shoves the hilt of the blade inside me.

He fucks me hard with the knife, only pulling it out when he's ready to bury his cock inside me. Colton wraps his hand around my throat, choking me hard as he fucks into me. There's a sticky warmth to his hand, I don't have to look to know it's his blood. My vision blurs, little dots dance around as I start to black out. Colton doesn't stop though, he fucks into me even harder, tightening his grip around my throat.

"Fuck that was perfect." Colton collapses

beside me, the sound of his voice bringing me back to the brink of consciousness.

"Yes, it was." My voice trails off as I start to black out again. Sensory overload kicks in as pain starts to spread throughout my body.

"Let's get you back to bed." Colton's voice is the last thing I hear before everything goes dark.

Fourteen

Colton

November 6th

Alex has been asleep for a few hours now. I left my dried blood smeared all over her throat, my cock throbs every time I catch sight of it. My bloodied handprint outlined across her throat is a masterpiece I don't ever want to stop admiring. She stirs in her sleep, nudging closer to me. Her soft snoring provides a soothing background symphony as I try to plan out our next move.

She's tried to fight me so hard at every turn, but all that's over now. Alex gave herself to me willingly, and there's no coming back from that. You can't deny your destiny, and no matter how hard it was for her to accept, Alex Sattorie is my destiny.

I'm racking my brain, mulling over a map of the country, when she finally stirs awake beside me.

"Colton..." She calls out, reaching for me in her half slumber.

"I'm right here baby." I toss an arm over her, rubbing her back softly.

"What time is it?" Alex mumbles out in her soft, sleepy voice.

"Almost midnight, you were only out for a few hours." I assure her. After all she's been through in the last week, I don't blame her though. She barely had enough time to recover from the incident with Mark before we went on the run.

"What are you doing?" Alex asks, sitting up more to lean against my shoulder.

"Trying to plan our escape out of the country." My response has her leaning up, staring at me with wide eyes.

"Our escape? Right...you're a wanted criminal and I'm your hostage I guess..." Her face falls slightly but she doesn't freak out.

"Do you want to decide where we go?" I raise a brow, eyeing her carefully as she thinks about what I just said.

"Sure." Alex smiles up at me with a grin so wide it makes her eyes crinkle in the corners.

Alex leans her head on my shoulder and together we start planning our future.

No matter what happens from here on out, I know we'll be okay.

Five Years Later

Colton

A stark white blanket of fresh snow coats the ground outside, it's almost three feet high now. The tree branches hang low, burdened with the weight of the snow. All four dogs are running through the yard, zooming through the thick piles of snow as they chase each other.

I'm watching Alex from the kitchen window as I finish cooking our breakfast. She's been out there for hours already. Tending to the farm animals is one of her favorite things lately. Watching her smile as she works her newest horse is absolutely heartwarming. They say animals can heal the wounds no one can see, and I believe that wholeheartedly.

When we settled here in Canada three years ago Alex was still just a shell of a person. Being on the run for two years had really taken its toll on her. It's funny how objects can have so much of your trauma attached to them. We decided it would be best if we burned the remaining pieces of Mark, I had gifted Alex. I recommended we get rid of the knife too, but she actually wanted to keep it.

I guess no matter how much we heal, we're both still a little fucked up in the head. That's what makes us work though, we get each other's fucked up shit and that's all that really matters. Alex and I live out our darkest desires with one another daily, and for that I will forever be grateful.

I wave to her through the window as she takes Maxine for one last ride around the pasture. I haven't told her yet, but I just found out from the previous owner that Maxine is actually pregnant. Even better is that she's due on Alex's birthday. Alex has wanted a baby horse since we moved to the farm, she's going to be so excited.

I'll spend the rest of our lives trying to fill that void in her life that was so horribly ripped away from her. Even if it means we end up with a hundred animals.

Anything to see her smile.

If you enjoyed Colton's story, stay tuned for the next installment in The Lakeview Asylum Boys. Your next psychopath is preparing to meet you soon.

Please leave a review on any platform that you use to review your books on. Reviews are worth more than gold to authors, and they are a great way for you to support your favorite authors for free! The places where your reviews matter most are; Amazon, Goodreads & Other Book rating apps!

About the Author

L. R Burke, (Lexi), has grown up and lived the majority of her life in small town, Alabama. She is very family oriented and loves to share her passion for reading with her little sister. When Lexi isn't writing away on her next masterpiece, you can find her either catching up on her endless TBR or cuddled in bed with one of her three dogs.

Works by L. R Burke

The Shadow Cursed Series

- ➤ The Secrets The Shadows Buried
- ➤ The Shadow Queen's Curse
- ➤ To be Announced

Lakeview Asylum Boys

- ➤ Midnight Mayhem
- ➤ To be Announced
- ➤ To be Announced
- ➤ To be Announced

Shop signed copies and exclusive book merch here!

Stalk me on all your favorite social media platforms!

Made in the USA
Columbia, SC
26 November 2024

47124171R00095